SIMPLE DEVICES

THE SCREW

Patricia Armentrout

The Rourke Press, Inc.
Vero Beach, Florida 32964

Patricia Armentrout specializes in nonfiction writing and has had several book series published for primary schools. She resides in Cincinnati with her husband and two children.

PHOTO CREDITS:
© Armentrout: Cover, pages 12, 13, 16, 21; © East Coast Studios: page 10; © James P. Rowan: pages 9, 18, 19, 22; © Julian Cotton/Intl Stock: page 4; © Horst Oesterwinter/Intl Stock: page 6; © Frank Grant/Intl Stock: pages 7, 15;

EDITORIAL SERVICES:
Penworthy Learning Systems

Library of Congress Cataloging-in-Publication Data

Armentrout, Patricia, 1960-
   The screw / Patricia Armentrout.
      p. cm. — (Simple Devices)
   Includes index
   Summary: Text and pictures introduce the screw, a simple device used primarily as a fastening device.
   ISBN 1-57103-179-0
   1. Screws—Juvenile literature. [1. Screws.]
I. Title II. Series: Armentrout, Patricia, 1960- Simple Devices.
TJ1338.A76 1997
621.8'82—dc21   97–15152
                                                       CIP
                                                       AC

Printed in the USA

TABLE OF CONTENTS

HOW DO THEY DO THAT?

Have you ever looked at a skyscraper and wondered how it was built? Compared to a big building, people seem very small.

So how is it possible for them to lift and move the heavy material needed to build these tall buildings? How do we cut and shape hard materials like rock, wood, and brick? And how do we hold it all together? The answer is **simple devices** (SIM pul deh VYS ez).

Simple devices are used to build our largest buildings.

SIMPLE DEVICES

There are six simple devices. They are the pulley, the wheel, the lever, the inclined plane, the wedge, and the **screw** (SKROO).

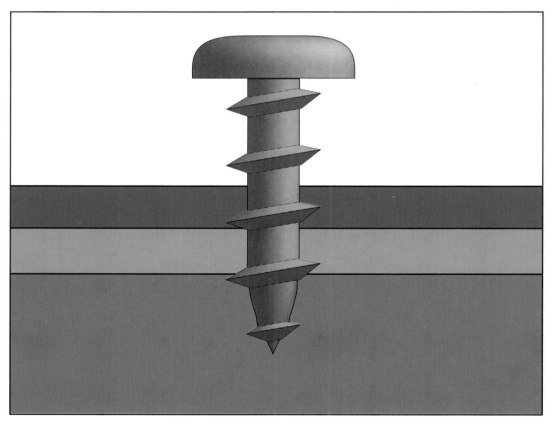

A screw is used to hold two or more things together.

This mining device is made up of many simple devices working together.

Although these devices are simple, they allow one person to do the work of many. As a matter of fact, when people combine two or more simple devices, there is almost no limit to what they can build.

THE SCREW

All devices are useful, but in this book you will read about the screw, an unusual simple device.

A screw has a head, shaft, and tip. The shaft has ridges, called threads, that wind around the shaft from the tip, or bottom, of the screw, to the head.

Screws come in many sizes and can be made of wood, metal, plastic, and many other hard materials. The screw is used for many different reasons.

The threads of a screw cut a groove which holds the screw in place.

A FASTENING DEVICE

The main job of a screw is to fasten two or more materials together. It does this job very well.

As a screw is turned with a screwdriver, the threads cut a groove into the material, making a hole. The groove spirals inside the hole. The groove holds the screw tightly in place.

As the screw passes from one material into the next, it holds the two together. To remove the screw, the screwdriver must be turned the opposite way.

A drill bit turns like a screw.

SCREWS IN THE WORKSHOP

The principle of the screw is used in many tools. One example is the **vise** (VYS). A vise is often found on a carpenter's workbench.

A vise can be used to clamp two materials together. A vise can also hold a project steady while it's being worked on.

Children like to play with simple devices.

A vise can hold your project steady.

When the handle on a vise is turned, it turns a screw. The screw brings a pair of clamps together. Anything placed between the clamps will be held firmly in the grip of the vise.

SCREWS THAT BORE HOLES

Some screws are made for drilling, or boring, holes. This type of screw is called a drill bit, or **auger** (AW ger).

A drill bit cuts through material with its sharp threads. As the bit bores deeper, small pieces of material are channeled up and out of the way.

Drill bits, or augers, are made in many sizes. Some augers are small, while others are large enough to drill deep holes into the earth. These large drills are devices that bore holes in rock and soil and help us find water and oil.

Offshore oil rigs use giant drills to search for oil.

SCREWS IN THE KITCHEN

You already know screws are used for building and boring holes. Did you know that you can find screws in the kitchen too?

Have you seen someone use a corkscrew to take the cork from a bottle? The corkscrew is turned into the cork. When the corkscrew is tight, it is pulled out taking the cork with it.

Take a close look at a screw-top jar. The lid has grooves that match the ridges on the rim of the jar. This match makes a tight seal.

You use a screw every time you open a glue bottle.

SCREWS ON THE MOVE

Without the screw, motorboats would float motionless in the water. You may have seen a **propeller** (pruh PEL er) attached to the motor of a boat. The propeller is a screw. The motor spins the propeller at very high speeds. The propeller

A motor boat could not go far without a special screw called a propeller.

Propeller blades spin forcing air away from the airplane.

forces, or channels, water away from the boat. This action moves, or propels, the boat through the water.

A prop plane relies on the screw in much the same way a motorboat does. Instead of forcing water, the airplane propeller forces air away from the plane.

SIMPLE DEVICES WORKING TOGETHER

The screw is a variation of another important simple device—the inclined plane. An inclined plane is a slanted surface like a ramp. The threads that wind from the bottom to the top of a screw are a type of inclined plane.

When you go down a spiral slide, you are sliding on a screw-shaped incline plane. When you screw in a light bulb, you are turning a screw-shaped inclined plane.

Now that you know how important simple devices are, maybe you can find new ways for simple devices to work together.

A spiral slide is a screw-shaped inclined plane.

GLOSSARY

auger (AW ger) — a tool used for boring

propeller (pruh PEL er) — a device with rotating blades that give motion, as on a motorboat or an airplane

screw (SKROO) — a simple device with a grooved track on its shaft

simple device (SIM pul deh VYS) — an object, such as a lever, pulley, or inclined plane, used to do one or more simple tasks

vise (VYS) — a device that opens and closes with a screw used for clamping or holding

The base of a light bulb is a kind of screw.

INDEX